T0196096

HOW TO BE
QUEEN
A LEADERSHIP FABLE

JENNIFER MAGLEY

ARCHWAY
PUBLISHING

Archway Publishing books may be ordered
through booksellers or by contacting:

Archway Publishing
1663 Liberty Drive
Bloomington, IN 47403
www.archwaypublishing.com
844-669-3957

Because of the dynamic nature of the Internet, any web
addresses or links contained in this book may have changed
since publication and may no longer be valid. The views
expressed in this work are solely those of the author and do
not necessarily reflect the views of the publisher, and the
publisher hereby disclaims any responsibility for them.

Any people depicted in stock imagery provided
by Getty Images are models, and such images are
being used for illustrative purposes only.
Certain stock imagery © Getty Images.

ISBN: 978-1-6657-0289-8 (sc)
ISBN: 978-1-6657-0290-4 (e)

Library of Congress Control Number: 2021902783

Print information available on the last page.

Archway Publishing rev. date: 02/26/2021

My life's aspiration in six words: I help successful people become unstoppable.

What is a leadership fable? A fable is a short story that illustrates a moral lesson.

What gives you the credibility to write about leadership? We are all leaders, and it begins with the ability to lead ourselves.

Books and Booking? Want to buy a lot of these books or book me as a speaker? Fabulous. Happy to help. We can also customize and cobrand *How to Be Queen* with your organization or event. Please contact connect@magleyjennifer.com for more information.

To those who suspect something is missing.

Have a story of how you overcame?

Visit: www.HowtoBeQueen.com
and share how you did it.

ACKNOWLEDGMENTS

Thank you to my ever-supportive queen mother, Evelyn Magley, for your presence in the valleys and on the mountaintops. Dad, thank you for believing in me since I took my first my breath. Jessica, DJ, and Daniel, thank you for making me a big sister and for your unconditional love.

I am forever grateful to walk the path blazed by indomitable queens who share my DNA and heart. Thank you to:

- My fourth great-grandmothers who were born slaves before the Civil War but saw their children gain freedom.
- My great-grandmothers Magnolia and Mattie, who raised ten and twelve children, respectively, to overcome during Jim Crow in the South. I kneel in reverence.
- Great-Grandma Rose, a Hungarian immigrant who didn't speak English yet raised eleven children in Indiana.

- Grandma Lillie, who was in the first graduating class of a formerly segregated nursing program.
- Grandma Mary for going back to get her high school diploma in her fifties because she had to quit school to go to work when she was a girl.
- My grandma Alberta for always rising so that she could get up one final time after her fall. I love you, matriarchs.

To my sons, Blake and Grant, you are creative, kind, and resilient humans. You know love as a way of life. I am proud to be your mother. You are greater than.

To my husband, Rob, I cherish you from the deepest part of me. Thank you for revealing the truth of how beautiful each day can be through your love. You never move the finish line. My heart is forever in yours.

INTRODUCTION

Fables are tremendously popular in the personal growth genre, but there was something blatantly missing in each one I read: me. Over the years of owning my own business, being a coach, and being a professional speaker, I never found a leadership fable written by a woman with a woman as the main character. I decided to take the advice of one of the greatest authors of all time, Toni Morrison, and leap: "If there's a book you want to read, but it hasn't been written yet, then you must write it."

Hopefully in these pages you will find the truth that unlocks the power to claim your crown.

— 1 —

After six years at the firm, it felt like I was running in place. While the speed and incline of my treadmill-like existence increased, I never quite seemed to get to my destination. Tare and Horace Capital implemented nearly all my ideas, but I still received cents on the dollar every other Friday.

For the first time since starting at the firm I was going to take my PTO, nine days in Italy to clear my mind with my best friend, Sam. And I was looking forward to it. She was flying into the city tonight, and we were to connect at the airport sky lounge before our red-eye flight. And then the 911 text came in.

Unexpectedly, our largest prospect could meet

with us in the morning, and as junior adviser, I was to come back in to craft the pitch, despite it being 8:00 p.m. This was typical. Tare and Horace would start off the night with a few inspirational stories and then leave in chauffeured cars, while we sat hunched over computers until the sun rose. It would be an all-nighter, but they had hinted at a promotion for the best pitch.

I had to abandon my childhood friend and would take the next flight out tomorrow. She would be devastated and try not to take it personally. I would chalk it up as yet another necessary sacrifice in my race for a title.

Despite a mountain of evidence to the contrary, I really believed that my pursuit of perfection would get me to where I wanted to be professionally. After all, slow and steady wins the race. And if there was one thing I knew how to be, it was persistent. For every uninvited criticism and slanted performance evaluation at the firm, I responded earnestly, determined to fit myself into their mold.

"Smile more. You look angry," they said. So I hired a body language coach, read twelve books on professional presence, and began meditating every morning.

"It's not what you said but how you said it," was the response to my pushback at a "joke" told by John. This gem of feedback prompted me to enroll in a master class taught by a hostage negotiator.

After that, for a better understanding of humor, I humiliated myself in a church basement with an improv troupe ad nauseam.

After being agreeable with a client who asked for extra attention, I was told, "You are not hard enough with tough clients." But when I gave a hard close during a pitch practice, they said, "You come across as too feisty," which inspired me to find the only silent weekend retreat in the city, at a former institution turned holistic hospital.

Finally, as though I could not be more aware and critical of myself, Tare asked, "Do you think you'll have children?" It prompted me to freeze my eggs. Well, that and the collective disgust from my dates when I'd mention my hope for monogamy.

At this point it's hard to know if my limitations are holding the promotion out of reach or their view of me as a limitation.

"Keep your head up, Elle," Sam texted as she boarded the plane. She was the type of person who cared. There was no limit to her nurturing abilities. She even bought and played vinyl records for her houseplants to help them thrive on a cellular level. Yeah, she was that person.

"I just feel like I should have more to show for the last six years. John just got promoted and he is years my junior ..." Seeing those words on my phone screen made me feel like I was whining. But it was the truth. The dangling of this promotion was the last straw I could grasp to see if they would finally recognize my contributions.

"Saying this in love," she replied. I could picture her tilting her head to the side and narrowing her eyes in search of the right words. "Maybe you can be the one to pitch to the client this time instead of John or whoever." She ended with an angel emoticon.

My chest tightened thinking of her on the flight alone. She was right. This would be the moment that I got what was mine. I would have the best pitch, and then I'd ask to be the one to deliver it. After they agreed, I would present and then hop on the plane savoring the sweetness of success.

Tare and Horace were already in the conference room as we wearily arrived at 9:00 p.m. With the exception of Ruth, our shared intern, the room was filled with John and several other guys with one-syllable names. My eyes felt a bit blurry, and for a moment they looked like the men I used to cut out as a child, each identical to the next, holding hands.

"Come now, everyone have a seat," Tare said with a twinkle in his eye. "Have I ever told you all what it means to defeat the bull?"

"Surely you have shared this storied tale, my old chap," Horace said, slipping his thin lips over a cigar.

The men shifted their weight, feigning interest as though they had never heard the tale before.

"Man was made to dominate," Tare began. This had to be the hundredth time I heard the story.

About forty years ago, Tare and Horace took a high net worth client to a bullfight in Madrid. The client became one of the wealthiest men on the planet as a result of his decision to work with our firm. The photo of the three of them, arms wrapped around each other in front of the dead bull, was prominently placed at the entrance in our lobby.

"We were made to dominate," Horace said, echoing him with a chuckle.

Tare continued. "And when that beautiful beast of a creature entered the ring, the matador was unafraid. He never broke eye contact as the bull charged him again and again. Knowing he was superior in every way, he stood his ground." He was transported, lost in the tale. "That's what confidence does.

"In the blink of an eye, the matador pierced the bull triumphantly. Then the beast fell to the ground, and the arena grew silent ... but only for a moment," Tare said lowering his voice.

"In that moment I leaned into our client and said the words that changed our firm forever: "You see what just happened? Let us slay the market for you, and you'll never again feel the charge of fear from the bull." Horace began to clap slowly at Tare's delivery, and the room erupted in laughter and applause.

"And that, is how you close a client, my team," Tare said with a dramatic bow.

I always wondered if everyone knew their tale was a farce. Quite literally, a "bullfight" isn't a fight at all. The bull enters the arena weakened by drugs and sandbagged with its horns shaved to keep it off balance. Petroleum jelly is rubbed in its eyes to impair vision, and before that, picadors, who are men on horses, drive lances into its back and neck muscles impairing its ability to lift its head and defend itself.

Slipping out of the conference room, I had to decompress at my cubicle before we started brainstorming as a team. Being this person wore me out. How many times had I barely recognized myself pretending not to hear a comment or silently accepting a backhanded compliment from a coworker? How could I ever defeat the matador when he had entered the arena after a lifetime of rest, and I was bloodied and broken?

It was in this fog of despair that I laid my head down on my desk in search of sleep. Some of my best ideas came to me during these naps before working until sunrise. Hearing the laughter filtering through the heavy doors of the conference room, I knew Tare and Horace had at least three more stories in their repertoire. Within seconds I was snoring.

2

To her surprise, she awoke to the sounds and smells of a jungle. Darkness was the only thing she saw, and its presence was all encompassing, like she had been swallowed whole. She tried to stand but fell over immediately.

"Hello?" she called out, rubbing her eyes. It felt like she was covered in fur. Elle's panic was rising; she had just been at her desk.

"Easy there, friend," said a voice from below.

She tried jumping to her feet but landed on all fours. "Hello? Who's there?" she asked, clearly shaken.

"Hops is the name," the hare said, looking up at her.

"Where am I?" she asked, backing away.

Hops, not able to believe their luck, waved a paw in front of her eyes. She couldn't see a thing.

"How did I get here?" she asked, beginning to pace back and forth. "I was just at my desk and now?"

"And now?" asked a new voice.

"Someone's with you?" She dropped her head to hear the voice far below. Sniffing, she placed her nose on his shell. A turtle!

It was far too confusing to figure out.

"Maybe we can help. Look, I'm a rabbit. What's your name, kid?" asked Hops.

"It's Elle." Her head was still spinning. "And did that turtle just talk to me?" It was absurd asking a rabbit this question.

"Poke, they call—" There wasn't a chance he could finish that sentence without Hops interrupting.

"His name is Poke, like slow poke," Hops completed for the turtle.

"Please," Elle said out of desperation, "I need to get home. I have a very important pitch." She paced back and forth. "It's my last chance to be promoted. And I missed my flight to Italy with my best friend for it. I cannot be here in the middle of some jungle, not able to see a thing, talking with you animals."

Hops looked at Poke with a sinister grin. Although the most unlikely of pairs, they had swindled their way into the final round of the annual race for the crown. The winner would be the ruler of the jungle. Ironically, though, they had been too busy celebrating their advancement to the finals and were going to be late to the race. The only way they would make it now required a faster mode of transportation.

"Look, there's a race, and we are on our way there," Hops said, circling Elle. "Thing is we are late. Maybe you could give us a ride to help speed things along. I mean you can't see anyway and don't know where you are, and we could help with that. Like a trade?" Hops said with an edge.

"Yes, and then we will help you find your way home," Poke added.

What choice did she have considering her current options? "Sure," she said. She'd do anything to get back to the office before sunrise.

A jolt of excitement went through Hops and Poke. "We have to grab our things. Just sit here for a few minutes, and we'll be right back," Hops said with a spring in his step.

Heading over to their bags, Hops and Poke began to whisper. "She can ruin our chances of snagging the crown," Hops said, putting his paws to his head.

"I ... don't ... think—" Poke began at a snail's pace.

"Cut the crap, Poke. It's just us. You don't have to be in character anymore."

Poke cleared his throat. "Well clearly, if she knew what she was, really who she was, we wouldn't even make it to the starting line." Poke reached inside his shell for a cigarette. "She never bothered to ask what she was. It's like she does not know."

Looking over at her, it was hard to believe. With her sharp teeth and sheer strength, her kind was top of the food chain.

"Do you think she would want to be, ya know, queen of the jungle and win the race here? Seems like she just wants to get back to wherever she came from?" Hops asked nervously.

The sun was setting as their plan began to rise. "If she doesn't know what she is, we have to keep it that way," Poke said indignantly. "The key is to feed her lies about what she is and wear her down so thoroughly that she doesn't believe she is worthy of being at the starting line."

Agreeing, they slipped back into character. Poke snuffed out the cig before packing their things onto Elle. Not being able to see what was going on made her nervous, and when they came back, she was relieved to have them as guides.

"Now, before we help you out by navigating this big jungle for you as we ride on your back, there are a couple of things you should know about your type."

"My type?" Elle asked curiously.

"We won't make you go too fast being that you are *so* big," Hops said with accentuation.

"Excuse me?" She was offended.

"No, friend," Poke offered. "Like … too big to be as out of breath as you were when we found you."

Elle swallowed hard. She could not remember a single thing besides being at her desk.

"The thing is," Hops said, circling her, "you're just too large and bulky to really have any actual speed. Which is why you would really hate being in a race. And you know, your type—"

"Not the smartest," Poke interrupted with a drawl.

"A bit dim at best." Hops tilted his head in sympathy, "Which is why you make for a great vehicle of transit," He concluded and climbed onto Elle's back, winking at Poke.

They didn't weigh much at all, and she was grateful for the company in this foreign jungle. Her desire to prove her usefulness, paired with the draw of being needed, felt familiar. This always seemed to be the currency in getting to where you wanted to be.

Between their shouted commands and general fogginess, she barely noticed where she was going. However, at each village they passed she could hear animals scurrying away. It seemed as though they were afraid of something.

"Don't worry," Hops assured her with a laugh. "They don't like outsiders."

3

Sam was certain not to make a sound. She was a rodent after all.

"Psst, hey, wake up," she whispered into Elle's ear.

Elle had fallen asleep to the sound of Poke's and Hops's laughter by the fire. Panic shot to her head as she realized she was still in the jungle and dependent on these two guys to get back. It was so hard navigating a place she had never been, especially when she couldn't see the way.

Poke had said they were only a day's journey from the race, and then they would show her how to get home. She wanted to escape this nightmare and be back in her old life.

"Hey, really, you should wake up," Sam insisted, nervously glancing over her shoulder.

Elle lifted her head. She had to know who this little voice was. And why was she so persistent?

"The others say I am risking my life trying to talk to you, but I know the truth." Sam let out a big sigh. "I can't keep watching these guys do this to you."

This comment piqued Elle's interest as she lay on the ground. "Risking your life? Why would you ever be scared of me?"

"Well I'm not because every mouse knows that we are safe in front of a lion."

"What?"

"Basic Jungle 101 really. We know that it takes the same effort for a lion to catch a mouse as it does a gazelle. So why would you waste your time eating me?" Sam asked, throwing her tiny hands up.

"Did you just say I was a lion?" Elle asked, jumping up and pacing side to side. *Could it be true? But how?* She had to know for herself.

Her heart was beating rapidly. "I cannot be a lion. No, no, no." She said, her voice sounding more helpless than before. It was one thing to be in the jungle talking to the animals. It was quite another to be one.

Recognizing her panic, Sam tried to anchor her with some questions. "For starters, you are pacing. Don't lions do that?"

It was something Elle always did when she was nervous. That could be sheer coincidence. "OK. And what else? I need hard facts here."

Sam cleared her throat. "You are like covered in fur."

"I repeat, I need hard facts." Elle shook her head, unconvinced.

Sam took in a deep breath and released the truth. "From your teeth to your tail, you are sharp in every way. Your senses are intuitive. Your movements are smooth. The whole jungle knows you are powerful. Animals often run away at the sight of you.

"Hops and Poke are using you, and they only try to suppress the ones who threaten them the most."

Sam paused at this last fact, waiting for it to sink in.

"It's not enough. I need proof." Elle almost roared. "Isn't it obvious that I can't see a thing?" It was all too confusing. It just didn't match what Hops and Poke said about her type.

"If you follow everything those two say, they'll have you believing you're a mouse," Sam said. "Have you always been this way?"

Elle plopped down on the ground, overcome and unconvinced. "What way?"

"Unable to see yourself?"

4

They reached the starting line right as the crowd shouted, "Go!" As Hops and Poke took off, Elle was relieved to know she was nearly home. Her conversation with Sam had literally opened her eyes last night. She could see, but things were still blurry. What she knew for sure was that those two would finish the race and then tell her how to get back to the office. And yet, something felt off.

The mouse had been so insistent. "Now that you can see, run the race and become queen of the jungle. Beat those guys at their own game."

Queen of the jungle? she thought and chuckled. As though she just had to check certain boxes and then could reign. Her time at the firm had proved that was a fairy tale.

In her world, being queen required Elle to be someone else entirely. Exactly who that person was changed moment by moment, depending on who was speaking. It seemed that life was much simpler in this jungle.

Suddenly the thought was a question: *What if life is fair here?* If everything were clear, Elle could win the race because she wouldn't have to try to be better than them. As a lion, she already was. Technically she was a queen of the jungle by birth, but winning the race would prove her worthiness. Sniffing the air, Elle trotted off in the direction of the tortoise and hare.

"What are you doing?" Poke asked angrily while crawling toward the finish line. "This wasn't part of the deal."

Elle could hear the cheering of the animals in the distance, excited to have a new leader. "It was a bad deal," Elle answered angrily.

Poke tried to pick up speed. "My dear, you needed help; we needed help. It was based on leverage."

"If that were true, why discourage me from entering the race?"

"Don't you have an office to get back to?" Poke released a spiteful laugh.

It was all over his face. They had lied to her from the first moment.

"You don't know how I can get home, do you?" she asked in shock.

He shook his head. "So now you've got it figured out," Poke said sarcastically.

"Seems that way," she said taking another step in front of him, more determined to win the race than ever.

"You're only half right," Poke called out as she picked up speed fueled by the thrill of the crowd.

To savor the moment, she slowed and dramatically stretched her paw toward the finish line. It moved away from her.

The crowd gasped.

Thinking her eyes were failing, she took another step to cross over to queendom.

It moved again.

How could this be? With each step forward, the finish line was just out of her reach. The faster Elle ran, the quicker it moved away from her.

A loud cheer of celebration erupted from the crowd behind her as Poke was hoisted into the air. Turning around, she trotted over to them, abandoning the moving finish line. How had he won instead of her?

Seated on his tiny throne, Poke called out to her. "As I said, you were only half right. There was nothing you could have done to win this crown. You see, the race is twice as long for lions."

"**H**ey, you really should wake up," Ruth the intern said, tapping me lightly on the arm. Yawning, I stretched out my arms and drowsily looked around the office with its stale lighting. The jungle was long gone, and everyone was filing out of the conference room. I had been dreaming.

Grabbing a pen, I wrote what I could remember:

The race is rigged.

It was around 3:00 a.m. when I closed the door to my apartment, squeezing between my packed bags to get to the bathroom. They had chosen my idea again, with someone else pitching, again. Maybe it was the disappointment of being here instead of Italy or flat-out exhaustion, but I felt defeated.

All I could think about was that dream. It really was how I felt. Like they were feeding me enough lies to keep me chasing my tail. Their feedback seemed legitimate, but how would I know if it was valid if I didn't try once more. I'd heard of gaslighting, the act of manipulating a person by forcing them to question their thoughts and fundamentally who they were in personal relationships. *Could this have happened to me professionally?* Splashing cold water on my face, I looked in the mirror. *Can I really see myself?*

Over the years I had bent to fit into what they said I should be, regardless of how it felt. At the beginning of my career, it seemed like my path was a jungle, where the guides had their own races to run. If you weren't an asset to their agendas, your presence was a detriment. Was it possible that my type, who I was on the inside, was already enough?

I had to know the answer. Rushing out into the street, I ran at full speed back to the office, my bags dragging behind me. It was time to take their advice in full force before catching my flight.

Entering the conference room, I gave them a genuine smile and knew I would always remember the surprised look on Tare's and Horace's faces. It was a half hour before the client arrived, and I took the opportunity to pitch them my idea, the one they had promised would grant a new title.

"Well, Elle, this is a pretty aggressive plan coming from, um, you," Tare said, looking over at Horace "Never thought we'd hear something like this from someone like you."

"Like me?" I asked bewildered.

"Look, this is a great strategy. It's just the implementation could be a bit difficult given that the clients will connect with John at a more ... how shall I put it"—Horace paused—"organic level."

"So you like my idea but with John executing it?" I asked, my heart falling.

I pictured the tortoise and the hare climbing onto my back. It was a fuzzy memory, but I could see a finish line that seemed to move with each step forward. If I were already the queen of the jungle and my business acumen, drive, and original ideas were enough, why was I trying to run a fixed race?

"No," I blurted before I could back out.

The color drained from Tare's face. Horace began to cough loudly.

"No," I repeated, unsure of what had come over me.

"It seems we have a feisty one in our midst, Tare," Horace said, searching his pockets for a lighter.

"If those terms are not satisfactory for you, my dear, and you feel precluded from the process, you are welcome to take your talents elsewhere," Horace said bluntly.

It had been years, and I had played by all the rules. Whatever there was of me to give I had gifted to this job. Nights, weekends, early mornings. My job reigned supreme without boundaries over my life. I'd wrongly thought that I would advance this way. Right then and there I finally saw that they would never know my worth. And that I didn't need their recognition to be a success.

"Well then, it seems that I must get going," I said, turning and walking toward the lobby.

"Welcome to the race," Tare shouted as they both laughed heartily at my departure. But in my heart, I had just crossed the finish line.

It's hard to capture the exact feeling I had sitting on the plane. I'd like to believe that saying no to them meant saying yes to me. Never had I been so convinced of a decision yet uncertain of what came next. Surely in my future there would be other firms, and turtles, rabbits, and jungles would never be in short supply. Yet what I knew for sure was that a queen reigned within me regardless of the results of any race. And that was more than their title could ever give.